bone bite snare

bone bite snare

Michael Mc Aloran

ERRATUM PRESS

ISBN: 978-1-7397708-5-3

First edition.

First published in 2022 by Erratum Press
Sheffield, UK
www.erratumpress.com

Design and typesetting by Ansgar Allen

(...*it see none sees elsewhere it cannot...blind sees less lesser see what from...black see none of what sees less of what...cannot see less what of for a...hilt depth trace see widen never...begin what from sees less absolve... what sees absent lesser breathes of it...sees black of none till havoc see ash oceanic seen...see claim what breathe aches nothing ever...see non-see...see what what matter of it... tidal-non asks what no answer to...breathe in-breathe... see asks cannot follow it... it is nothing or...wind absence of tide sees only end... end of follow mark hollow cannot it claims none more arbitrary...withered see says what no answers to...sees left no distance right...permeates of none sees eclipse of shadow once...matter see matter says what undone to... to answer to says none distance ever... locks blood as if it too were to decide it sees...recollect what matter... oceanic nothing amber nocturne so & as if to...still breach ask of it or not of what...lung lapse of see all eye unseen...silence/ silent/ silent traces...sees what is not sought...unknows of breathes allsame...denuded eye what of the seeing of it...lacking of the lightless seen/ ever-elsewise...fragments traces nothing for tomorrow's absent flame.../echo/ echo/ see what null...gouge of all closed wound absorb sees/ echo/ unsung...ask now of the why to the too of the why of no question other than where zero the closure eye that once where knew silently divulged as what lapse of passage play & silence weighted in the palm of the other then returning to the other & so forth as all that in-between of the what steady nothing to be in the absolute cast aside in a breath of dispel an end to what flourish yes what an end to become of it to make of it it-dreamt of finally nothing of the furthering the lessening the…as too soon the door ajar & the jaded shadow shed left behind as if to breathe of it were to be of in an elixir of vanquished the night no further step once two/ stepped not once…)*

...echo singular count of/ zero echo count once whisper murmur neither/ bones unto forage for in-dreaming next to follow breathless by design/

a strand of blind light a garrotte/ broke jaw bone blood to wrestle stolen from desire's chalice-tide/ shadow-ever nothing clad in pelts of skin-deep laughter echoing verandas of night's claim upon/

sudden yes or no sudden to expire till taint white ashen stolen from gardenia effortless/ lock-stun of unknown pageantry/ a whisper recurrence no/

unsaid unspeaking collapse seasons damaged nullity collapsed lung of sickness dwells in parched throat/ what winds to grace the absence of/ sky not known/

here or there walls warp in a cast of dice syllabus a mockery of silent effigies/ zero cracking apart/

resonate in marrow-mind ocular roving a foreign drift till taste of razor despair given to piss upon all terrains/

dragging out/ a corpse of tide lapses ever in bound bones effortless unspeaking of/ plumes of burnt blood till count none singular/ Ave/ nothing taken from begun...

…eye sky a little shod black bitten silhouette stung-lapse of/ in/ ever of/ collapse in-dread forage null till bone shatter bruised bloody fleshed veranda give or taken/

silenced/ absence of/ till colour-claim effortlessly designed desire for (the) one thing seeking vibration tones/

lock-trace/ a caress/ sheared skull blessed a relapse nothing given nor taken it/ out-stretched wings a kiss of cold sands where no sun is birthed/ funereal tide/

dead what once/ fades out once more in paradigm of shit/ dread lock once forgotte the broken body of signature/ slashed wrists here now a sanguine trace recollects/

(in night to trust)/

onward says (the) naught/ din of cold closure a doorway dragged from listless tidal/ oxygenate of nothing ever some lapse or another's claim/

breeds pageantry silences working till hollow tint a painted trace/ outro/ (steps once diameter ever no motion beyond)/

peeling final from stricken blood/ ice in (the) veins/ eye neither eye spied upturn in lock white overture…

6

…vacuum pitch colour(less)/ stone wind breaking upon fallen exigency an echoing veranda of absent wave/ devours devour/

draped in meat I-bone collective rot of singular sun +1 collapse/ nullity sunk zero in abattoir tears blind weight knocking uponexcise till wind's expire tread what once/

once more/ laughter echoing through the pores of parched vertigo/ again what as if unto to be a subtle in of which eye-clad salt in wound/

…/ stun-spoke/…/

waxen all/ psychotic tread given to birth from an ever flowing none/ speeches trinkets things for some other absence/

cold weight of null and void seeping in where fallen tread redeems no light broken upon emptied soil/ fingers to dredge in fleshed obscurity/

walls as if there/ walls warp in (the)/ in-suffocate of no clear distance calling from what black till nowhere left to be/

blood beneath butcher's fingernails seclusion not a trace/ breaking broken locket of final ever/ no not a…

*shrift wind till understray a shard a shive of bone snare
reclusion effortless demise to fever itch cold stone exile(d)
shadowing…*

…black bite snare/ beckons of/ blood still as/ cleft the sheet-wind's overthrow/ of what else as if to/ sting-shadow lights/

bereft of/ clemency of the naught to follow/ as if what said till claim of the beseech/ asked of/ flesh gathered in pit of longing/ said without/

murmurs of dead speeches/ the bitten un-flow of exigency/

veins taut/ effortlessly cast aside the break-neck following on from/ into the non-dreaming of else spoken as of/

blight non-sight a circus animal's beheaded laughter/ echoing/ final as/ as if in the tearing of meat given to taste at ever-eclipse/

heart lung what breath the breathe is held/ scatters the dead bones long forgotten/ as if to claim where there is none/ as if to folly unto/

all speech erased but for the slivers that mark the surface/ from the surface swept aside by the empty-handed lapse/ bone snap of where does the lapse reside/

asked of/ night yet night cannot be/ films coat the eyes/ in the drag in the drowning dreaming else/ no nectar haven/

snare black bite bones withered/ walls from which out of which/ nothing to claim/ reversal/ static overlay + 2/

desire/ desire for the blackened atrophy of some voice that never dwelt/ sky upon sky upon watermark/ in the light of the spun carnage of innocent…

...snares it cannot be the bone lock of the teeth/ fingers reduced to wilted seasons/ white ash/ the movement from none unto.../

given that the taste devours/ scream-white never without end/ whittled the light limb occupancy/ clarity is for wastage/ of the shining eye's address/ stung which way or other felt/

skeletal as/ carousel/ bled-bleed of the bitten tongue the mock resound/ it is nothing it cannot follow/

bitten the asked of violence of the snare of teeth that slaughter motion/ scarred upon till afterward/ the scars recede/ they never recede yes or no/

bone black the charred scratches the walls are dissipating there was never it was ever thus/ until/ mocked yet by the lung that refuses silences/

taste of spit/ bloody asphalt/ the machinations of desire in the glistening blade/ across the flesh drawn the glistening of till bite/ the excess of which uncharitable absolute/

thus speaketh the lie/

bound till excess/ turning whatever next into nothingness/ not a trace nor fragment other than the callused pulse/ spitting out the claim of paroxysm/ let it slide/ there will yet/

undone for the sake of never having in spite of/ drag of sky yet of/ else of what yet till have or held/ skinned the ever-flow/ tactile as ember upon/ in exile nothing ever…

…the bitten lapse/ stretch of obliterate/ of dead silences/ crack crack there go the bones/ nothing as exiled homestead/ the words coagulate as if to choke/ a light bulb shattered & then gone/

treads the emptily of/ spasm lock/ the vapours/ vapours arise as if to drill the final into flesh/ the dreaming then is of/ (not achance from the…)/

locked headed as of sky/ film of emblems/ emblems/ the eyes are blood they are smears of shit beneath the sky's abort/ not a trace but for the silence/

tone deaf stone or/ gravitates towards the lapse only to find the lack/ black stone grate/ the chiselled teeth of night glow amber in dark corners/

pelt of never-forgiving emptiness/ no solace in the recoil/ coil/ recoil but 1/ comes and goes the voice mistakenly/ a virus pageant/

played out for the given of a lifetime out of the lack of anything else/ the embers fade/ the seasons laugh louder yet growing dimmer of ear/

the chalice mocks the carousel/ all/ dice cast in a winter's corrugation/ the barren veins kiss the dusted chalice/ tidal of/ in the glare of the long forgotten/

bask of/ stretch of obliterate/ what of/ paring away the skin away/ bled out/ until.../

voiced yet without purpose/ scattered emptily the words graze the surface/ no darkness belittled/ no silence overthrown...

I

...a slaughter of in any given outcry where to nothing of is to excise skinned landscape desolate as echo of whereto of the collapse is to burn of stripped black meat as of what will in razor recurrence in vault of exile to where bitten of is to be snared in the silence absences to taste till what matter colourless appeal some drag some scarred as was risen from electrical nothing of to bear as vacant the eyes cold vibratory light of locked to ever/ unto...

… (a taste of veranda a broken lock a lightless pageant… skinned flesh opening up a corridor of scream given to vibrate of wailing in an outcry of the blood…motion of lack of motion collapse of bitter waste taken from once begun…the hand that reaches for yet recoils from edge of recollect a shiv in the breath of secret flesh… nothing to burn of all thin as lights to bear down upon a silence never before known throughout where to mockery is of some bitter skyline…all lapse of throughout where children play upon fresh grass as barren of to advance is all that be in microscopic colours…trace of the absurd long shadow of devour…night recollect where to birth is to abort from any given roomscape desolate by design… glass to shatter in a realm of unknown savagery as damage seasons collect the shit of plenitude…spoken of…never once of it…vital shadows burn into from out of reach…blood to caress upon denuded skin)…

…a blade a smear of flesh upon clear glass flies gathering a vacuum of where to bleed is edge closer to some ultimatum of final excursion throughout which a sickness to occlude bone bite & a bitter frenzy teethed to the sky alone as of what held driven nails in flesh echoing out some gilded sarcophagus of dissipation where to follow of is to nectar breakage limbs chamber of eyes ablaze through vent of bleed of shadow's ice…

… (discharge of waste of cum upon a cold bodily obscure blood run cold no longer of it in wound seclusion barricade…roomscape of scattered bloody petals of some desolate flowerings…ashen vapours arise from some depth long hollow abortion pilgrimage…trace of blind waste a sickness of to tread throughout nothing closure tongue…broken limbs litter the pathways of beyond …night's vengeance is to remain silent birthing merely through some bankrupt vocalise…cold spasm of uttered prayers from depth unknown…echo-echo fade to resurgence skinning the breath till fury bound … nothingness picking the scrags from its…blind cataract eyes stare out into non-space given to invert…catascope of final given unto abattoir a-bleed throughout ablaze… castrated lights to spill their shafts upon nothing ever as was shown to forget it of throughout…dead as…a strip of film torn from obscure visions barren as)…

...a breakage from till glint in foreign lights as from what speech deliverance to taste what lung of some obscure tasteless design of skull slashed through by silent reek of light dissolve taken from yet given to where to be outreach is of for into where fallen sky merely of nothing of to bare it to the longing silent laughter of breathless murmur of where to be obsolete laughter echoing in silent tongues a birth-ed landscape ablaze throughout it...

…*(a trace in the night of gilded opulence…a child's dismembered limbs adorn the desert sands as of debris…breathless redeem of disintegration venting to the sky as if it mattered a fuck…prayers from the deep to strangulate…ripped flesh from the gouge of mouth to birth dead longing in a pitch dark night of alongside it breakage to…silent whispers from…endless origin of beseech…slashed wrists of amphetamine striations … psalms to some image long lost…dead all foreign of as if to have where speech is closure as…light fades out from origin of forgotten sunlight…the blood cannot be washed away it seeps from the stitched eyes of dead purposes …nothingness to pare away the bones as of stone wishes for…electrical…doused wastage of flesh to caress…ablaze in the realms of echoing vacuum kisses…skinning the membrane of its quality until fade a silhouette…burnt light a kaleidoscope of excreta a severance of meat)…*

…severance of distil in an effortless ablaze in shadow's realm where to sudden as if to outcry is to nothing of as speech eclipted dies down to murmur echoings through some absurdly locked to breach from ever less than having been in raw red rush of blood where fear to tread is of some behold catastrophic flood of echoing of distant rooms drowning of some excise to grip as of teeth to the throat cutting the air from vital all sung snared unto…

…(a feast a fucking famine of remembrance vibration tones dead as never having to of mercury night fathomless abort of…the sky ripped asunder is to grit of teeth a focus upon where centre-stage is to bloody waste… evacuated broken shells of having been in shrapnel tears as was were…distances given to naught…digs deep into flesh the fragment of ice to pulsate in ravage silences…nothing of the spoken word of eclipse it long follow…utterance utter lack of all disclosure sung aloft from some bankrupt edge…skull X.d out…vacant stares collect as walls warp & shift & distance ever- of caresses the wound…bled haven of jagged terror to build in an offspring of prism catascopic…a rush of blood to the…nothing of of vocal broken of what as if to follow steel edge come to fore to sever…light X.d out…banquet ablaze in the tributary flesh…eyes melt as of blood upon dry sands ever to follow less than ever was before)…

...striation of wound to expel where countenance of given atrophy is to break from listless obsolete given to devour the sickness of as if to disclosure fathomless absurdly cut of the lie breakage havoc dispel of rotting syllabus from one dead air unto the next where silence ever of some abort is to close upon the pulse gripped by the sun it to climatise is to shadowing birthed as of from one room to an other than as if to in absence of silenced by...

…(one singular breath to champion the finite lie as once till known of a smear of teeth catches in cold light…fingers warped by drought reach out into where to having been from the outset is no matter of…vacant attrition of blind weight some sarcophagus of dreaming hence as if to… insects to swarm in the realms of sleep division a caress of razor aptitude…flesh melts from the bones reveals the havoc of bone stricture…dense wind of shadow knocking upon the eyes as of slumber's silent echoings…fragrant distances stretch out across the floorboards an exhalation of silver smoke…lifeless all what given of to taste the attrition mark of sufferance lapse of to in nor of collision fathom…dawn to strike where to voiced of is no consequence…light extinguished utter dark…a theatrical motion of intrinsically devoid to break no ever of as will in which to ever of long shadow…silentium to caress a lack of bitter sting of haven lack where to of in now/ or)…

…utterance of bled lack overture where to of is no longing for ever of the bite of final excise skinned to the teeth of silences burning cold weight of distance a candle extinguished nothing of to be head vast underwater skull where to break broke skin a-bled sudden as if to recollect as the torn meat laughter of before scattered dead lapse of unseen traces of lifeless pageantries through what dim a doorway unto abandoned landscapes all foreign as…

...(scuttle of dead waste where to naught is of to bled a sky marked by the scar tissue of some foreign night ...effortless demise where to spell it all out is to burn black ice of forget it colourless...oceanic the edge of blood at the edge of discarded light...stones cast as of obsidian shards unto where to of what of it...from outset...nothing of which to see in a coil of detritus & shards of bone weight...eyes that turn from utter dark as in the upturn colours the like of which never before witnessed...black blood to seep from every orifice...a warp of flesh a burning effigy...steel to taste upon the tongue whereof what longing for nothing left of the marrow's edge...pared down the meat of it obsolete... ennui of broken lapse a drag of carcass to touch lights abandoned frozen in blind air...suspension of...walls what once of vacuum chamber no longer the of wish fulfilment...a final grip of an invisible sun to break upon where nothing of is to be)...

…sufferance blind there is no light by which to view the corpse of memory buried in the meat of collapse dead tones of breathless turning throughout where to vault is once stricken from the dusty sheets of silent traces of nocturnes bled out burning in thick heat a vulture's trace a foreign bleed eyes to touch where to bone is to collapse of entity salve in autodestruct of carved flesh turning upon a breathless close of wound it unto shadowing…

…(strips away the cadaver reclusion in the tar of broken glass & rust metallic silence of obscure detriment final as of some expel…teeth to bear down upon in thick white air perhaps smoke there is no perspective…one singular distance…never on yet to the brim of it solace of excrement rubbed into gaping wounds of tearing…a discharge a weighted breath…long corridors of absence lacking in exit signs…birthed terse into never having asked of it…lightless as…torn from one wound unto the next as if to avaricious…confessional vapours unto a silent audience…genuflects before a vacancy of shit… scattered bones of the once known altar before which to ejaculate…blood's trace to realm to bite down upon a cold dark chalice…septic light & the sting of alcoholic demise…nothing there…ever as…razor speech of the silent edge to caress as if to salve breakage nonchalance… it long done…it of forgotten laughter/ of)…

…broken shadows in a collective of meat to bone to tragedy lack of it turning upon where to of if not what silence of throughout birthing the fleshed close of hour upon hour as if to asphyxiate cold hours of exhalation at the pitch of it black echoings of excise to response is of in now what measure taken from to bleed of some sarcophagus tears to shed breathless haven of desire for the one thing adamant of light discarded as of refuse…

…(shrapnel of the birthed once the unknowable traces of absence of where to bloom is to cut away the flesh of it given to silentium…sleep to burn of in bloody sweat a distance to breakage bone lights…effortlessly lack of colourings…a discarded carcass sinks into frozen waters the throat slashed…a child of time perhaps a mockery of…night to burn of in electric tidal opulence a reek of shit of some impaled lack of…aptitude…cold cut of to the bone to the marrow no blood to floweth of as of speech declaration lapse of light…trace of vapours tones of some forgotten chamber echoing of vacuum havens… solace emptily to burn of…a deserted landscape where to nothing of is to become…yet still yet shadowing as was ever no truce with the silence of it that emanates yet has no form…voiced dead from the onset of it… collision of extricate…till seeketh of what of till nothing of abounding in the null of being in an echoing desire for final as)…

…of it to taste blind speech of the fading trail throughout the flesh a stitch-mark interior of bled corpses silence all the while till breakage from what spasm lightless abort a turning of some effortless striate burning at the pitch of dreaming vicious to expel it speech of none a long distance of ever of nothing from which to turn from eats of the broken body vocal as was once till closure eye foreign as was once a traceless dreaming of what sky to…

...(spurious metals of disease...a razor's caress in utter dark...blind weight of a slash-mark promise given to disclosure remnants of cold air to stick in the throat's foreign bodily...shaft of light a broken jaw a broken column...stretches out an infinity of singular intent...a quarry of meat of sufferance...coal dust in the lungs some reaching purpose...silence all the while a nail driven into the membrane to convalesce as time's absence to reek of it a bitter solace from...nothingness forgotten a cold blank landscape of soundless tears...cuts close to severance the breathe of it to spill blood...dead tones of vital signs...pulse rotting spit of vacant absolve... fingers that recoil from the outstretched amber dissolve of...sees eye it forgotten...remarked upon some burning welt of silenced ever-traceless lacking any motion or origin... snared of throughout by hyenic laughter talon of the unsung...step non-trace...echoing footsteps)...

…falls away the eye of which a silence of throughout in some mercury dawning ever of to bleed as once was breathe-d nothing of the cold broke solace shattered to obsolete as given of the bone dust of a desire for nowhere of distance of till stricken lapse a closed fist a torn from as of eye spat out into some useless foraging given to having been remarked upon burning to be in an absence of what known nothing ever if nor what till close of it…

…(builds from the absence of collision yet lack in utter of a spent force…a taste in the mouth of bitter ashes blood to spattered across the gait as echoing of it fade of light an absence of scene…dissipation of…detritus to define… shadowy nocturne of frozen blue mists across a lapse of distance…an open casket of loveless feeling… in damage seasons of…spits in the face of it cannot nor of broken haven…takes from what sense to collect the fragments of it…nothing of the matter to be… ever of the…traces of…blind lack of tumour eye… taken from…speech declaration of…nowhereon… dense recollect…savage the traces of through a decline of ever…a bodily flung to the emaciated rabid dogs of speech…skinned tidal oceanic… breathless as… laughter echoes throughout the silence an echoing of… distilled light to extinguish as if it ever was…nothing of the matter to…nothing ever if nor what of it/ an unsung devour)…

II

(…from the commence of never a light shone blacker than what once ever other than as fleshed of silenced as pageant nothing ever a rip of gnaw upon emptily enshroud in earthen calamity of blood never a step taken more than ever was before bleed all edge what foreign then nothing of it from out of distance what else to bare bear awake once less then less than ever given unto taste what helm of it discards & then another if it matter less than ever once then of cold shard of nothing as if to have of emptied out of presence no no nothing of that too close too close to touch it strips away to nowhere bound little choice but to all said what spoken of nothing of it yet of in nor of once more what matter if or other than that was ever once before

*else as of which reclamation of unto in lack of distill rips
shreds shadow lock of night irredempt colourless thankless space a blockade yet no nothing of that what as if to
whisper traces no speeches no all forgotten mimicry of
some vague distillate no no longer wishes to seared light
a foreign absence of sound lack in all its cannot lapse
light leapt closure no of wound bleed out of tidal weight
collapse deft breath devour no hope in hell grace as if
to ever no nothing there a hand that clasps eternal as
one is not second to go is first flog of some lack what
over then of some accord all spoke once more there goes
it tidal no yet given to speech reclamation in laughter
of some hung light afar afar that reclamation never of
where once to be*

*waste ground where now the closure of what given
to beckon of as if to speak all days done for haven no
what of till colourless maxity stray says no yet of what
origin bulk of which weighted what of till tidal as
forgotten nothing of see another there appear to be hours
without wonder a drift of cloud across pupils long absent
skylines all what sung as if to know barrage of silence
severed flesh bone deep an absent frenzy of night & all
that it obliterate of lack of frugal of poverty bones beg
for change lights to obliterate as on it fathomless fleshed
in or out yet never truly of collapse into what din
speechless cycles of recurrence of silences stone nothing
all it undone lapse what all in of what in nor of what
foreign subtlety frozen as of which what dawn*

silence of expel of intake of night to elapse where to once what of elect to din of soundless echo echo nullity blank space tone dead lapse of eye until whereby of fallen shadow long vacant ever of closure of some nothing ever there in an absence of/ where to recoil breakage no what term of dislodge collapse shudder shatter wordless soundless broken never answer tidal atrophic lapse what long & all what sung from derelict absolve lack of intake desire for once that never other ever than obsolete devour colourless in laughter of which a collision bathe in black waters closed shores where flesh abides all fallen forage no all forage fallen nothing to remark upon lapse all to having in dread of hour upspoke forgotten of in lapse of else some distance none

no there what once never as what yes or no cyclic as solace
ever in what else of which given to recoil where once was
haven of disclosure never of yet of where once all spoken
no yet yes as bleed it all from severance severed to bone
sharp reek all sung as if it were nothing of which zone
of which whereof till closure entity meat to unspoken
of redeemed till lapse what forage weight of eye where
breath once of whereof silence allwhile drag weight
what of echo-echo what of what now in of where to
be is to where none abounds parameter distance is shit
in one's shoes drag of it all have it all at a loss suffocate
of entity breathless a room lack taste wherein of which
where eye is of the stun forsaken spoken for forbow…)

*…in an erasure of blind trace of it into taste of razor
ashes breathless as once known silentium of final edge…
of shattered lights collapse echo tremor forgotten bled
from*

*once sensed until foreign of or…trace of shadowing
upon meat no longer forage for in or of silence(d) as
was ever as once more…drag hence taken as of which
from out of*

*reach given to redeem lack lapse of all once saying of
now none…ocular roving colours trace of distance lack
where to have is to dissolve landscape of nothing/ ever
as…*

*…absent breath as all what fallen ever of some nothing
once sought finality of excursion as if there ever…given
to unto as if to never once lapse in thin light scars cast to*

*flame of which what or other of…forever night from
which to null & voidal collision into passage from flesh
to liquid traces…swarm lack to caress taken from what*

*speech dies down it to of which nothing of what better
of…excursion into lapse longing echo-faint as blood to
raw cold silence as of butcher's blade…*

…as for of no nothing there in shades of night forage
follow of breakage of escapade eye alack…neither to
speak of cast aside as of debris scattered words upon

barren earth(en) final as before…tones of which that
clamour for half-light birthed from breakage point of
haven merely an end in sightless…it cannot be advance

where to sculpt of night cuts shadows upon bare fleshed
desired of silent as once known…spit of broken laughter
to terse nothing of it what claims to behold throughout
cracked glass prism…

…secrets to set to light in voidal incapacitate whereof
in lung set to light cancer flowerings gather in denuded
eyes…till dress what dawn in rags of disappearance

claimed from hence it bleeds unto throughout in or of…
silence tangent nothing of to broke is to stun dark haven
night where all is lapse lack of some design…long

forgotten an outset of foreign distance throughout where
fury pageantry closes its fingers as if to choke…noose
pilgrimage of scattered petals of frozen blood upon rind
of meat long distance absent of presence…

…wound's outcry is to be in or of what matter foreign sun no matter fingers to reach for as lens fades to zero eye…nothing to then of in throughout where to of is no

matter hence all is dead as final eyes…black tar to ever know of it in closure of what lung's desire for cessation all yet nothing for in taken of…of/ upon/ light to rot as of in

throughout to trace where to have neither of nor either if shaft closes in mind…as all what all that once was soundless echoes in blind space in cataract design where all dies down…

…elixir tidal of motion lack taken from given unto electrical fury kiss of cold stone artery…dressage of fallen sky upon where flail upon flail is to elected to burn

blackened as…pares away throughout cold solace absent reaching for of some nothing of in void dissolve…spills blood of vocal eye never of throughout to reclaim what

matter of some absent longing for…it all done for says of it in or of in final echoing from future tense as tears to brim in eyes that have forgotten…

…hands fallen of it to never have ever once neither of some reclaim colourless appeal…psychotic winds caress where to fleshed is fleshed merely sickness of to thrash in

shattered membrane…terror at/ at pitch bleak haven asked of no not a nor of nor else nothing of which to lay claims upon…salt in wound of vacant attrition another

pulse another escapade of bedamned lights…in an escapade of shit where only of it to be redeem of solace nocturne closes it hyenic flows freely…

…all locked to echo's dim forgotte(n) seal of eye there another here another in vacuum chamber undefined …ever to of nor naught reclamation distance of which till

close of hour slashed through given to expire…nothing of it of in what else to follow in drench accord close of hour to sever once again…it long dead as of ever said once then

thrice distant all as nails dug into flesh to grip a vulture tearing…as all in weightless flow of eviscerate of nothing where to closes wound drag of heels throughout as if to…

…in an obscure end of flight what locked to meat long shadow fallen to nor if in out of fury pageant closes… burns of ending in an effortless disregard where

to strip from lock of eye trace of electric pulse not a… till burn what of there is no trace of want for better excursion taken by maggots what are nor of which… all what gripped

throughout a vellum parchment drags alongside where to dense weight lightless abort…all sung for some stretch of spe/cial never to be defined as floweth counter-throw taken by non-sight…

…unspoken hours to claim whereof till bitter pips spat out in gait of unrefined stone decree…all solace never once breaking from hilt till shattered glass overtures made to

unto if at all nothing more…never of whereby what of cold light to rot & ultimate disintegration a throat slashed …ever of to/ not a word no not a trace where spoken by

is of some corrupt blind effigy whispers in utter null … what or if no matter of it till close of wounds for some syllabus reflect given to distance no nothing ever as…

…taken from what given as trace alongside closeth no contract breathless harvest collapsed into…as dreamt of less than of through gutter tread whereof till obsolete a

scrag of excrement of nothing…broken as of which as neither remark upon cold shadow of eyes upon through silver haze unto…nothing claimed from nothing to

reclaim through silent winds terse as blood is stubborn until bloodless final…mock of itch stitch of redeem throughout what spectral desire to final weightless sung as of for neither of/ in…

…drag of caress of absenteeism & all that what once never of throughout attrition wastage tidal…ablaze as if to echo of it fades out null void & silent gathering of winds to

collect ashen footprints…observe of eye alone neither of remark given to trace throughout some dense or other fragrance ever of…as spells it all out in a mock lung traipse

gilded light eviscerate by final listless ever…ever of some nullity factor of breath dim quantify of light that emanate from stitch of wound to burn of it…

…breath emblems nothing as before where to warp of sheen cast before as kicked of shit veritable knock upon…all said what longing for never having been yet

other of throughout where to motion throughout distance trace…eye alone & bitten of throughout whereby no place for it in or of what matter close of wound to…sung aloft

from indescribable lock of stone closure what realm of which where to be is of nil & ever…flames of which gathering in pelt of sky alongside trace of lapse of none spoken haven to destroy as if it…

…dirt kicked up frenzy reek of birthed from out of which ever as before neither of nor passage of…of caress through ghost-limb tongue some savage desire for

utterance yet cannot in pageant fury of which…all what lapse of which into of given eclipt as echoing to leak from every porous exclamation turning aside or of…flies upon

bloody waste pass through given fleshed disaster colourless appeal yet rank with silences…mouth agape solace of mesh through which bile escapes ever of through which some collapse of…

…in skinning pit of never of where to rock some cradle of graven thought to opiate sleep is in neither of nor breathe…eye seeks to settle never as before as fixed of

gaze upon where sky is of abortive wound of sun…as of/ dust brushed aside no matter as if from ever dissipation of collapse into frozen yet of ever of…longing to weep

from whispers language of forgotte where to by what else of fade of out listless desire…close of nothing ever of where to lock is of to ashore knocked upon where to vertebrae sickness of to dredge…

…frozen wastage of night glorious paralysis of dust fury echoing of marrow ablaze until it final ever… extinguish of eye of body vocal edge neither of some lacerate through

whispers dead tones…collect of blood beneath butcher's fingernails echoing laughter of some damned reclamation …in vacuum chamber silenced of in allwhile other than

process of reclamation bile to cast upon…shit-deliverance of through skin's absorption little what of in wastage of unsaid knocked asunder stray…

…breath(en) flux turned to whisper warped womb of white heat sarcophagus of froze white tears…ashen promise of all of forgotten ever of what traced before

through warmth or otherwise lack lapse given ..focus of intent upon where to of is to fragrance of elected to this/ broke stone tragedy of cards cast no…await of dawning

into to become of some never having been or otherwise decide it otherwise decision null…feeding frenzy of hyenic final laughter as if to mock what tread is of nor other claim or no what from/ why from…

…distance no rooted to given to speech declaration bloodless night collapsed into of which until…tidal opulence of blood come to shores of till dread of which

haven lack all shadowing devour…colours of which of absence tidal oceanic spillage of breath where to embalm is to nothing ever…waste wounds terse where to closure

space lack of definition one singular edge to caress razor silences…all at once unsaid to drift whereby cold drift of broken amulets seeketh from as night impenetrable/ bite down…

…crest to fall upon where to shiv is to breathe spectral as given in shadow timescale of desert clime absent of… sky no linger taste of ashen promise where of in now of which

flat-lined eyes that seek to utterance collect…lime quarry of searing membrane shattered glass pane of transparency inept as ever once of other than…cold

weight to lack other of through which dispel seeketh solace drought of echoings traces burnt to dust…as if to/ all but once never favour of adrift skull compress sequence of riddled flesh meat to tear throughout…

…cauterize of once cannot neither of in final as seeks semblance to taste nothing of being-in emptily…drag of pelt across absent landscape stone clad as burning of

where flesh to be is sickness of where to nullity… bankrupt veins a/ motion lack of absenteeism where to having birthed once in absentia in reek of blood's tide…calls

cards they are spent as rotting orchids adrift in some foreign breeze settling in distance obsolete…breathed to un-sky trace of lock-a adrift speechless as of once ever of some shadowing collects in din refusal…

…echo to trace reverberate of skyline sieved by fingers cold dust of voidal exigency of bereft light end till none…lapse of throughout shimmering of halo tread of

limb warped colourings bite in darkness overture… vault to breathe of effortless to crush in thin lights subtlety of blade to caress in fleshed abandon…eye see eye sees once

or other scattering of embers in detritus breathless of to burn of it knock silhouette…silence bleeding out where once was of sustained as of in which till of what of in or less than as nothing of…

…obscure distance no longing for to burn as of blackened meat dissolve spasm tread throughout gild of absent… razor slash eviscerate to hilt of ash an evacuation

of shit upon dusty sheets…blood to lack as of some colourization as limbs once foraged die down in listless slaughter…mock of stitch of some reclamation

taste of desire in haven of where to flesh is to absolve is to breakage…subtle cold light as if in which of uttered blank space point of light to fade as of pupil's invert…

…inter-spasm of line drawn white chalk through spacial lack of definition mercury of shimmer bleed… dredge of in nor of gouge of mouth stretched before unknown clad

in pelt of nothing ever rind of breath…scarred without longing for to settled within of spoken unto where none of being is of else in dreamt of…spoken of what shiv to

trace throughout where to of abode blackened sun light absence of sky…corrected if yes or of breath shredded of purpose other than through as in tint of blood electric…

…carcass eye of genuflect from outset laughter echo-long spattered shit across defunct walls…syringe breath of nails in meat stripped to warped light escape of essence no

collision memory…amphetamine vibrate of steel cuts to bone of eyes ablaze solace realm of rupture lights…peels away skin of breathless opulence to reveal where pulsate

of meat of sarcophagus entwine…spits realms from none given to abort where freely of is burn nothing of in that nor otherwise adept of…

…in or of in of call of cards dense meat & absenteeism in fury pageant locked to once dead algorithm…silence

all of in as of where to embrace is to shock preference
of being in…marrow discharge of excrement in veins
bound

tight till collision shadowing what of…hyenic as of bled
in vibrate thrash of mercury of bloodless silver clasp in
specious recollect…climbs to veritable heights neither of
reduced to silenced realm of discharge echo echo…

…heave from out of which psychosis film upon
membrane of silt of breath of some never recorded
utter…reflex tide of spilled cull of shit blood cum & piss

throughout where to be is fall silent dead shadowing…
streaks of sky of night birthed from fingers made to rust
made to burn of it in pale light dim as before it…
mirror

mirror of before in which to view some detract silenced
dead as a lie…hands dead foreign kisses tread what
will from outset nothing of some ever-was/ of…

…colourless traces before which some simulacrum
presence of no design clear cut wings of breathe…eye
alone it transfers through silenteeism pageant in foliage

of spent blood of distances no longer…process as if from
drag it hilt in vicious detriment elected to nothing

breathless piss upon an open wound…till dredge what

closure tongue ripped from gait of powder-white bone white drag of terse…obsidian flower death severance to call out into where echo of to be is never answered of…

…clasp-knife cut of some breeze to descend upon as if it had never once throughout mocking of…striation of breathless ripped from a castration of tongue ripped from

some banquet of fury unobtained to offer…false solace of breathe of pulse blood fathom collecting of in or of where scum division a-bask…lightless realm of spacious

invigorate silver diabolo reek of silence in all as of in never ever…dense as if to say that/ collision trace of specious collide where to of is to final picking scrags from silent lightless as…

III

...oblivious to the commence here there or barren ashen sunk white knee-deep in shit-reek there was something what was it named after the fallen sun lapse there here or hereafter as throughout what spoken what was spoken never once through there till breach abandon colour it whispers as if it were a trace through empty cavern placement semblance of spit it out collect of bone wither silence no guide as of it all what specious laughter turns into gutter's refuse the fingers that trace the surface indent of what never throughout given that one could there or if to clogged an artery a fissure claim break null of void of dim recollect in a distancia of obsolete never yet known etch upon what spoken as if to detrace strays from pathway one two or other through pathway cleared by bone implements nothing of it the papyrus of the tidal of all clog out in forage forage it-sense rock paper scissors a bitten snare of black a caress once more through utter dark a hand appears draws back the surface where from it recedes indent no the surface regains winds a mock tongue rhythm close the door it cannot nothing ever there cannot in a vice of some tomorrow laughter's trace breakage what light a crack where though weeps through to scald the mockery of the once was known the once will ever the once to be until/ as of it along what traceless haven Ave repeat after me Ave parts the traces with rupture fingers cold abandon spits it out a deduce meat none broken stone tablets a trace of excise as all what fathom no it closure

around the throat a bind a syllabus a noose a scorpionic falter dense as a congeal of the blood's relapse fallen unto waste whereof skinning the eyes to bitter sting of obsolete (echo) oblivious to that final cleft below the rib oozing bile a taste of iron or shit in the mouth through prayer it once none done nothing cannot fully ascertain undone…

…of in that of which what of in that cannot as through a glass shadowy reflect an etch into of where meat is silent there hung in suspend neither smeared yet vibrate glisten of dead blood wind asway tear bled alongside as bask in none where through non having ever have as was before sunk of eye where to hollow gouge whereof some flourish null where being is borne down upon by rat & broken of in body vocal absence catastrophe where sickness to dredge collapse it is break nothing ever as before pulsate in night denuded reek of cold zero reflect in none where shit is beneath skin's travail a carousel laughter bread broken fallen to precipice as crack whip density of rind a deathly silence marked only by extract by blood an expulsion of weight's collect in tyrant membrane an echo of desire for some noose's pageantry throughout where night is furnace nullity sees eye to eye with cold chamber zero cracks apart nothing ever as before a subtle as never was bleeds slowly walls astringent traipse footstep taken one before another circular as is/ matter of which taken as before as light genuflects & finds no solace in from glisten stead a shattered vase a bouquet of frozen orchids & stone winds breath as was once until neither in as of what from said when piss for blood is mark a stone final upon cascade of night's embalm as on & into ever floweth null stop collision rat surfaces to forage breathe of cannot expel it is choke upon at silhouette's silent edge draped across bodily where form has long abandoned it never of in

exile subtle deaths to taste where absenteeism stitch close breath in useless penitence where broken traces & lapse in or of throughout thereof desiring of as in what till a trace of meat a mockery of flesh a passing remnant what hilt through zero cold reflect as rat breaks bones & takes from taste till ever of it what & never of some placement ever in through which lack stance breakage colourless appeal where nothing has never of has ever of through fallen lapse kisses with fragrant meat the collective shat lapse of it is a lie almost even in throughout or of another of in terse of closes it behind as outstep into nothing ventured fallen unto wayside cold shadow reflect a forgotten birth as if where collision nullity is by mark & precipice merely of another hour another bone flung upon where pyre obstruct silently devoured by as it were to ever of...

..silver beech reflect of blood soundless echoing vibrate of surface carrion kiss if atrophic scar alongside never as of once of the before reckless seed of collision abandon detrimental nothing all what once till dreamless speech absurdly unto mock of harvest a wastage of bone step one less than haven echo dim in trace seamless caress of hilt dredge body oculate ever as of which whereby what forage mark smooth calm a breath(e) devour of meat dense skull riddle it this neither of remark upon cold tidal blood reflect of subtle as of never bitter the pips spat out the teeth to follow cold dredge in laughter lung lengthy as of foreign closure solace nocturnal forage nothing of the decimation stretch till pageant Ave nothing of stares down reflection of a fresh cut razor blade reduct stillness broke stone barricade unhinged cold density desire for the one thing ocular fade/ erasure foreign forward trace collision nothing of to trace ever to expose where henchman no/ till utter dark...

…candelabra of human teeth skin of the blessed remark a fruition of dis-ease cast from which till restless devour colours of which spread from haste till given solace restless denounce a landscape of devoured light caress of one neither of recount once less than opulent seamless fingers to touch where shadows graze or dissipate into where solace struck what trace absurdly mocked a grave dug nothing of what once spoke shatter elixir as final all what uttered was of nothing collapse into where broke(n) limbs eclipse…

(...*they are the hyena's children mocked by silence
enviable worst less broken bodies ruptured in thin light
exodus fall from reach till adrift through corridors of
barren-toned abandon* ...)

...livid lived broken stylus an open wound of sunlight cracked through neither of the redemption/ nor the gash-mark sneers tasteless derision of the...all attrition nothing of the redempt skull wrack eclipse extinguish it extinguish the...

...dead zero whispers frenzy silken bathe all murmurs the dead traces an embryo of silence spat out elixir fathom of non-speech it collapse into what linger nothing of shadow-breath(e) it haven un-skull it bathe white senseless sentient expel...

…thrown to the dogs for surplus meat in havoc density reduct closes fathom door expose of glass surface blind by silent collision breath it-dream/ nothing tilt of glass exposed teeth that glint in white light shadow-stray desire for the one thing never have of skin the fingers reach through divine tension…

…breakage a thrown stone away from nothing from to begin from commence the longing absent skinned apparatus till dream-like haste expel of light cut by some rarefied cloth know to wipe away the shit the bloody sexless butchery of weight given to absolute…

…nothing said of the mark the forage attrition reap of steal through night it rhythm noted given to unto what silence force-fed through the endless night's devour as was what once soundless in-dream of which to scar upon scar a pathway through where none what once silence as was once as in the beginning there was…

…once was a gift a run of the expulsion trace without bread broken experimental dust wipe away a sheen to follow nowhere on where farce upon welt upon farce the broke stone worded as before never of the limb torn from either dressage of nocturnes perhaps ritornellos one cannot fathom much of the so much of the…

(…skinned so much as before…peeling shadows from wounds that weep the tears of an auge of desire for the one thing absent as the skies cannot…)

…it upheaval solace scar a solace scarlet…nothing ever there as once noted was the priority a waver of where landscapes clog the lungs with bloody shit…repeats after me/ Ave/ deduce the bones the skull's ashen flowering expel a turning in the absent fingers come to wrench the night from silver coinage…(it all once know)…

…reflection of long storm clouds image of immense sky & the extinguishing pulse at the edge of prayers long lost long cast aside where to breath(e) no nothing folly absurdly mocked/ waters never once yet of to blindly of it neither of to run clear…

(…hands blessed by tears by prayers of the warm breathe of intonation jagged as broken glass a raw rip of razor kisses the specious absenteeism spat out a wound lack of purpose farcicate absurdly mocked by…)

...dream what once of the sleep of neither rest the nocturnus given to lockade to bone marrow traces silver the absurd tint a glint mock till turn circular in deep scarlet roundelay shadowy stretched across where benign dust rusted purpose a cigarette blossoming in the dark where once what of given to benign served not once where tidal is fallen upon fingers outstretched to embalm with night the silhouette despair of breath a smear of might sudden flash amber-red from out of the depths till end as of claustrophobic sickness to kick from lapse to aptitude of reckless scarring of the singular the second the third all spoken as was once trace of desire closes the hands no longer the ashes in wounds that bear down upon like jaws to freeze in erotic valve convulsed till tonation a footstep taken a silence & a nothing more...

…all from what lock to terse given as of frozen lights bloodless silences a drift of calculations spun from till obsolete claims of the broken solace ill-rapture disclosure sudden in outcry a taste of bitter meat till said what of bound by sudden climb in outcry sentenced as what once obsolete what of till more that unknown it-dread of…

…point count in division of where to eye being of what closure spill of vertigo stillness to breath to breach to closure fist what matter lightless shadow of shattered glass a shadow birthed from oxide nothing of the before-here the now-ever as to hint where to bone exposed where limbs extended gallows' shadow a dream an exodus…

…a flight from echo into foreign echoing desire of ramparts a fist to pummel the skyline's teeth of glint through shed once dream stripped of haven skin in laughter of frozen by exigency as torn at by the given hyenas of being as rat from poison-lapse the crotch to devour it-fallen nothing as before in solvent accordionic laughter blind…

…fragile beat of it there it goes the fragmented light breaking through from out a return till tillage clean obsolete as stone edge paper scissors as before…scald of the upturned eye till steel it-entity frozen waste of ashen promise tilt at the edge of spoken for…

…have of once as broke body skeletal redeem nothing of what matter ever of in tone-white grace a skull to empty of through content set alight…laugh-it of what once a syllabus of wounds of terse skin say what of it done dead as no it a slap to the face again restless yes it…

…last call of frugal wasteland given that what whereof in tilt spillage closure spiel of electrical charge a numbness a black ball blind given to upturn whereof it-speechless the light of thine eye…as sawn into two three or four ritornellos of haven speechless turn from writ to the shit in one's mouth the movement from taken as written a silence ever…

...spliced where once(d) echoing of the bled sky's line carving the attrition break long absent irredeemable collide with nothing bartered for inescapable expiration from wound's desire it sheer cold culpable extricate emptying out the skull of breath beneath it is said mocked from pillage dread of yet breath of once spoke the colours expire as of so much wandering in through out of nothing ever the vocal smiles a carved gait of the long shadow breaking broke null asking of through vocal bodily broken as if all speech denounced what was into the merciless no merely the observe of some solace nothing solaced closes the eye till filament dissolve what spun cold as it is dim yet of throughout some drought sharp removal of bleeding out unto no turning from what dense recollect effortlessly ever-ever spoken of what voice what as if what once was said throughout forgotten in an instance breath digging up the fossils as if shrapnel tears where once were once no nothing ever it in the lung till spasm trace weight vapour tones & the blight of flourish next till poverty of in the downward tread into what is of some dark landscape absent of all redempt close to what in if what spell nothing's chambers echo chamber of spiral piercing inwardly of once what was in the becoming closure depth what surface what sentience vibrating throughout through obsolete irredempt mockery of tongue foreign depth through static binds electrical promise & the sunk occluded throughout echoing out as vapour traces once

more a pathway through till the colour point enters into
through vague distance mercury throughout the long
shadow having fallen vaguely reaches to touch to taste
still yet as once was lightless boundless once what matter
here once then the beckon forth till closure echo's light
fallen effortlessly clean break the bone revealed through
the meat of din collision nectar sediment expiry not once
nor ever having been not known as if it were uttered
through the body vocal sudden as if to trace calling
upon inversion stripping the lungs from out of echo's
reach through sting throughout cold chamber of rot the
words broken as were once nothing coagulate where
from what dense throughout given to expire still yet
biting upon the blade of excursion no longing for excise
a foreign taste of irrespective thankless ecstasy of the
what once known through it as if akin to having said
when all else fails where lungtish colours the breaking
breath skied once till absolute it what once was an it
& on goes till strike a match the bloom to follow where
lilies once blossomed exercise of demise where solace
naught redeems the cascade of till collapse in given to
expiration broken soil dried blood & the turning of
the shovel in it as if to say that once that it mattered
as through what sung strung aloft through the echoing
disease or retrograde where to taste is of the dead light
what once it will return bleak solace headlong broken
as if to redeem given to expel bile blood shit cum & piss
as if it mattered not a trace the fade unto out whereof

cold shadow of never having been once said the recall
of never having been ripped to shreds echoing breaking
throughout in silence solace din what light bending in
the eye that is the revelate as it were as if to once more
where closure fist is the ambient seclusion one singular
circumference one singular wall in which to echo-echo
drained of ever expiration in the fallen lightless through
the fallen lightless voice garroted on its own terse willow
excursions what once was shredded blind chamber of
endless lack spits them out the shards of broken razors
in din of dark through the broken body vocal trailing
behind through the language of the body mutilate
skinned as if where to ember is to recollect skin-deep
throughout delving into which the furtherance of sky
what wind collapse drained of all things permanent
other than the sky aloft shifting from azure to cadmium
deep tidal nothing further to bear as once no not once
other than yet not once it was never thus fallen from
what grace that never was coiled around the centrifugal
exigency abandon lapse and the warmth of the blood
that never flowed where seasoned terse reclamation
fallen of the misgiving what of it all called ashore till
bite what dreaming of in next till aftermath where
flesh is what of it it is what flesh is what of it longing
after through the lack of finding nothing in it other
further absence a recoil beyond the dark into the black
through mortuary breathing forth what syllabus cast
off through singular what as if as it were the echo of

once more recounting its losses to the crumpled scum of density found to be when one finds sentient occasion dragged from kick and scream throughout once echoing out through silence permanence the drought throughout cold chase specious demise some colours claimed through speech-clad reclamation distanced from the without where night is long and vocal does not abound it spoken for the only & the speech of claim the rest said with what privilege the meat tearing away from vocal shadowing as once what was where blood tones speak the rhetoric of nothing ever shine a light the birthing of what once tidal oceanic ever-what closes the wound expires throughout the drought of what to bear closes the final eyes of sleep forgotten merely to slumber long into ever echo where night is ever ever-long…

…wherein precipice of design is the culling of the once was vocal throughout where some glad sentence as if to cast were blank shadow spoken unto no-one no-thing nowhere bound it speak drowned parameters as if it could through broken valves of feel dense abounding as if to suffocate shrill to touch that cannot be that can only sever where blood is solace the cold lie nothing further bounty of disheveled teasement elected to this what once now burning unto absence fingers itch for the unsung desire broke stun & the turning reaching outpouring sudden to demise that may ever yet be sudden in outcry through colourless expiration stripping the meat where once a broken column of light breaks these dead waters flowing as if to gift the dark not a trace of ever having been but for some echoing silenced frozen upon surface dead tones the breaking of something other than what given unto speech circular expulsion a tidal breathing in suffocate shattered glass overtures throughout the culling of exigency giving it up for the prayers that mock the thin film of light coating the body vocal tide as once was said yet whatever what not a trace of ever-long cut short there is blood in the lungs to choke the bud the blooming breath drowned off through the blind eye's purpose collision nothing ever much to the point of zero's claim as if it were in that once was the body vocal nullity of cracked frozen flesh where opioid caress solace as what throughout what dense glimmer tidal wastage of bones furrowing colours close the door it is already

sealed shut to the reek of it where nothing drips from evaporating fingers of the dreaming lessened never yet once to clarify speech impediment of grace as was once dead it speaketh throughout the joy of night fissure taint collectively opens up the wound a trickle at first then the deluge of furious expulsion the sky dead the eyes useless faculties through the ever-sense of none as words cascade into the attrition dark what dark light what light the meat of it is the severance of opening out unto cascade spiral of exile alone for all time as if it could be other than ripping out the pulse bulb silence that permeates all things cannot shimmering breath the tone of the winds that cannot clasp having uttered nothing sudden to expire throughout where nullity stretches out its pelt through the ongoing unfeeling the cold weight and the rip of it excised from want till speak cold dice cast to the emptily unsung throughout which the vapours of all sudden to expire through futile break the sentient collapse where the sleep of agues bites down not a trace of desire for the exist through in of out then of what spun cold electrical frenzy what laughter long it breaks the ever-spun of nothing left to bear as if to erase the body vocal were to cull the vacant desert of design it will end as it begins it will commence when it expires such it is spoken of yet never a trace nor blood's final vapours the weight of flesh braces down upon throughout bodily to open up to the unspeaking vibration where given then through edge of flame cast upon cold shadow's *silent imprint slowly to shift across transparent walls as of throughout mirroring the breath dense yet even-sighted the longing of where nothing can only collide with nothing birthing plumes of ambient discharge through the depth of what once known through the eye's rip colours absent then where point is reached given to reduce where claim what will expiration & all to be uttered of through the lightless pageantries of the broken body vocal ever was from outset onset through tint speech absence of all spun alack through vacant laughter's waters drowned out temperate blood of empty rhetoric…*

…crack knuckle bleed exile trace of bedamned meat a sarcophagus of lightless smoke in veins a-dream it-shadow specious cause of what once aglow nothing much lest viper close of wound bedexed absentee so writ(ten) was the word clear skies an abort of sunlight cascade of the below whereof silent travail throughout never of the beseech of neither of the absurdly broken solace saturate in blood cum & shit of redempt nothing of the weight to follow it is a lie as was uttered hollow spat frugal taint tight travail where to absurdly mock of syllabic laughter the locked jaw of the bone bitten salvation snare that coil of neck-snap defecate deter where the shadow's internal organs turn to vibrant dust as if to worm throughout whereto of as onward broken bodies ruptured scattered nothing of the remaining of the collide it-depth nothing barter seed to scatter(ed) once was abandon all what words all semblant traces of the obscure the marrow's landscape a reek of acrid shit that carries through the vague light's distant effigies never knowing of the once twice thrice repeats after nothing on the commence of it to bleed one final asking of cold taint it matter broken nothing as of which till terse redempt nothing ever of the collision verge where coil of edge redeem spill of light to replace the internal collapse of having abattoir kiss taint flowers ever of the shadowing as if to density is to reduce to dusts nothing as before where once eye coil in desolate devour subtle as to of & which of out of to the…

…nowhere if/ return from broken blood asked of throughout the redeem the solace mutilation given of the burn to touch grace through the majesty of exaltation of absolve…light run low of dim reclusion…body a-mask/ denuded it is of the echo stone of the absurdly locked spat in the face again of from the before of the commence forgotten nothing of as if to claim of it embers embers null & voiceless…voice yes vocal yes words nothing vacuum tide & the shit in one's shoes a harvest of disclosure breaking from fever till fever unsensed…on no…rotted…rooted…vomits once more… what once more the origin of…all that can be sensed is the reek…& the perhaps twice or thrice by the second & third remark of it…skin the body whole… nothing ever of to the amass of it to nothing ever much of it is echoed…

…in a heaving stun of steaming organs slap down tryst sick bile etch of broke limb orifice collision electrify slapped down upon stainless steel skyline opulent silence give or take one thousand windows screaming their vault of tidal blood effortlessly obscurity solace a kiss of blade across the throat ejaculative devour staunch of woundage silver coin a-spin upon the navel frozen waters the depths of blood-rage fallen to crucifixion tones the like of which silence to repeat it merely of to get it over with it was once then enough of the other climb dead tense waters flowing let it bleed let it falter signature erased nothing of to mimicry dense as what once of the haven from the dug trench climate of rat pulse parameter see of in the once was fallen known of no more…of no more the gilded complex of fallen obscurity breathless longing for in the heave of this or other given to expire dusted realms of derelict rooms poisonous only of where nectar dreams of denounce it from the other scar of the lesser more than blood to excise skin upon skin to turn from demarcate breathless avarice a void of emptily expose of meat's devour of flourish regalia distant shadows to come closer closer damage nothing as before of the silt-traipse syllabus a mockery of teeth to snare through bone black bite to unto bitten reclusion in dirt whereof to cold stone dredge of corridors of aftermaths never of the detritus edge of the serrated kiss white shock light a forage a nothing a…

(...filters out un-sound/ sound/ given to collapse into other than what once/ drained vocal of/ or teasement of until nothing ember-lock/ harsh round of echo-echoing/ a path never cleared across/ sound eclipse till given snap what stun alack/ eaten of till shadow formed across exposed eye/ non-said/said/ from which all said all sun/ step un-step breath violet/ a glimpse of never what was ever was before/ before in asking of/ (fade out)/ final shiv in eye of percept/ broke bones/ sound given to retrace/ trace/ seasoned from pitch bleak lightless till given night/ in vertigo snap/ all/ sound simulations gripped by breathless/ soon to dissipate/ songs of un-being/ traceless violet songs in bloom/ distillate to point of never having been/ all purpose shredded/white lung till breakage/ a shattered tongue frozen of inept/ in echo chamber/ steel's lament rips pulse meat flowers from given density/ on and on it/ till risen once more/claiming that it can/ what sight what sound/ not a vulture's intricacy/ a shed of rat-black teeth in vocalise/ given to unfall unto/ bitter shards bite the eyes of sounding/ yet no lament for given loss/ white-washed wall/stare.../...ash unlock/ blind wither claim nothing lapse/ else no treasury what nothing settled breath/ unsettled/ broke catascope undue rigour/ breaks none of lapse sequential/ sound basking in sound of/ reverberate of unknown viewed from an externus/ it/ vocalised as if to/ endless streams of sound reverberating from/ surrounding ever unknown known yes or know/

no/ if quantify/ sound bile dream ejaculate of voice/ this is sunlight it/ un-sound of which the dissipating trace/ inhaled to touch nothing/ silenced once more/ coloured by corners/ blind lights/ none abounding/ sound evacuates of its own voice/ shears black/underwater skull/ prism promise of trace/ vapour lights/ excavative/ echo-echo nothing/ remaining/ shutter snap down/ escapade/ wind ice tunnel of/ dense what/ sound what/ interpretive alignment/ (says what it does not know what it knows not in silent reek of inutterable bound)/ evacuates break stone blind fed none/ subtle break/ in dead as lung/ sound wither/ scattered shrapnel tines/ abandoned to silence/ still yet silences spoken of in wilt of sound/ overture of nothing claimed/ frozen in/ clasp weight lack of/ not...white ash of sound/ settling un-silenced/ silenced in/ fundamental as shit/ inconclusive/ yes or no/ it posits as if to indent/ not a trace yet in blood pierces eye's unfold/ escapade lock/ stripped from out of echo/ glimpse in which/ knocks/ rejected by unseen un-sound/ nothing claimed/ not a step nor murmur/ none all stripped welcoming nothing more/ being nothing more in-sound/ yet utters what it can/ as if to parry/ it cannot/ so back then to utter blind/ light non-sound/ words terse/ no not fleshed it/ if it/ satiates nothing/ in bleed of lapse from until timeless/ once again...)

PUBLISHED BY **ERRATUM REPRINTS**

The Scourge of Villanie - John Marston